Magic Study